I AM YOU

A BOOK ABOUT UBUNTU

Refiloe Moahloli

illustrated by

Zinelda McDonald

amazon crossing kids

Previously published as *We Are One* by Pan Macmillan South Africa in South Africa in 2020. First
published in English by Amazon Crossing Kids in collaboration with
Amazon Crossing in 2022.

Published by Amazon Crossing Kids, New York, in collaboration with Amazon Crossing

www.apub.com

Amazon, Amazon Crossing, and all related logos are trademarks of
Amazon.com, Inc., or its affiliates.

ISBN-13: 9781542035668 (hardcover)
ISBN-10: 154203566X (hardcover)

The illustrations were rendered in digital media.

Book design by Liz Casal
Printed in China

First Edition

10 9 8 7 6 5 4 3 2 1

PUBLISHER'S NOTE

Ubuntu means "I am, because you are." The word *ubuntu* comes from the Nguni languages of isiZulu and isiXhosa and embodies the idea that a person is a person through other people. It is a concept of shared humanity, compassion, and oneness. This ancient philosophy is a part of many African cultures, including South Africa, where this book was first published.

When I look into your eyes,
I see myself.

I am you.

When I look into your eyes,
I see your heart.

I embrace you.

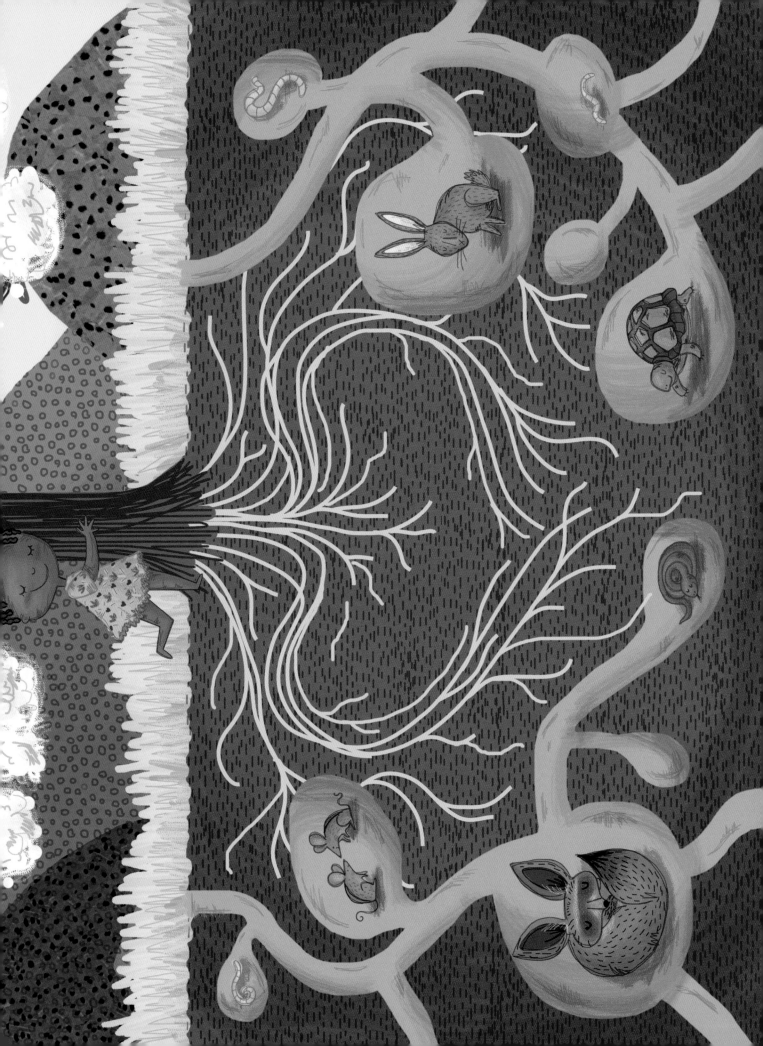

When I look into your eyes,
I see your beauty.

I love you.

And because I love you,
I love myself too.

When I smile as our eyes meet . . .

when I hug you as I say hello . . .

when I share what little
I have with you...

and when I walk home with you after school...

I love you, and I love myself too.

When I listen
as you tell me your stories,

when I dance
as I see you dance...

when I laugh as I hear you laugh,
when I hold your hands as you cry,

I love you, and
I love myself too.

We may look different,
you and I...

sound different...

Ons is een ...

act different…

eat different food…

and live in
different places.

But our hearts beat the same.
I am you.

To hurt you
is to hurt myself.

To tease you
is to tease myself.

To be kind to you
is to be kind to myself.

I am you,
and you are me.

I am because we are one.